Sophie and Jack in the Snow

TO
JOHN

Also by Judy Taylor and Susan Gantner
Sophie and Jack
and published by Picture Corgi Books
SOPHIE AND JACK IN THE SNOW
A PICTURE CORGI 0 552 523097
First published by The Bodley Head Ltd. 1984.
Picture Corgi edition published 1986.

Text copyright © Judy Taylor 1984
Illustrations copyright © Susan Gantner 1984
Picture Corgi Books are published by Transworld Publishers Ltd.
61-63 Uxbridge Road, Ealing, London W5 5SA, in Australia by Transworld
Publishers (Australia) Pty. Ltd., 15-23 Helles Avenue, Moorebank,
NSW 2170, and in New Zealand by Transworld Publishers (N.Z.) Ltd.,
Cnr. Moselle and Waipareira Avenues, Henderson, Auckland.
Printed in Portugal by Printer Portuguesa

Sophie and Jack in the Snow

JUDY TAYLOR

Illustrated by Susan Gantner

PICTURE CORGI BOOKS

It was getting colder every day.

Sophie and Jack watched

as the snow began to fall.

Soon it was quite deep.

"Let's slide," said Jack.

"Watch out!" said Sophie.

"Let's toboggan," said Sophie.

"Mind out!" said Jack.

"Let's build something," said Jack.

"Something very special,"

said Sophie.

And they did.

All afternoon the sun shone.

"Time for tea," called Mama.

"Look what's happened!" said Sophie.

"Good-bye, snow hippo,"

whispered Jack.

"Hallo, snow hippo!"

shouted Sophie.

Here are some other Picture Corgis you may enjoy:–

THE LAST PUPPY
  by Frank Asch

MOONCAKE
  by Frank Asch

BELINDA'S BALLOON
  by Emilie Boon

PETERKIN MEETS A STAR
  by Emilie Boon

GOOD MORNING CHICK
  by Mirra Ginsburg, illustrated by Byron Barton

JUMP, FROG, JUMP!
  by Robert Kalan, illustrated by Byron Barton

BARNABY AND BELL AND THE BIRTHDAY CAKE
  by Pamela Oldfield, illustrated by Jenny Williams

BARNABY AND BELL AND THE LOST BUTTON
  by Pamela Oldfield, illustrated by Jenny Williams